This igloo book belongs to:

....

igloobooks

Published in 2020
by Igloo Books Ltd, Cottage Farm, Sywell, NN6 0BJ
www.igloobooks.com

Copyright © 2020 Igloo Books Ltd
Igloo Books is an imprint of Bonnier Books UK

0920 001
2 4 6 8 10 9 7 5 3 1
ISBN 978-1-83903-379-7

Written by Stephanie Moss
Illustrated by Francesca De Luca

Designed by Alice Dainty
Edited by Claire Mowat

Printed and manufactured in China

FARM STORIES

igloobooks

Contents

Best Farm Friends

Hen and Duck were best friends. They did everything together, except on hot, sunny days when Duck loved to dive into the pond.

SPLASH!

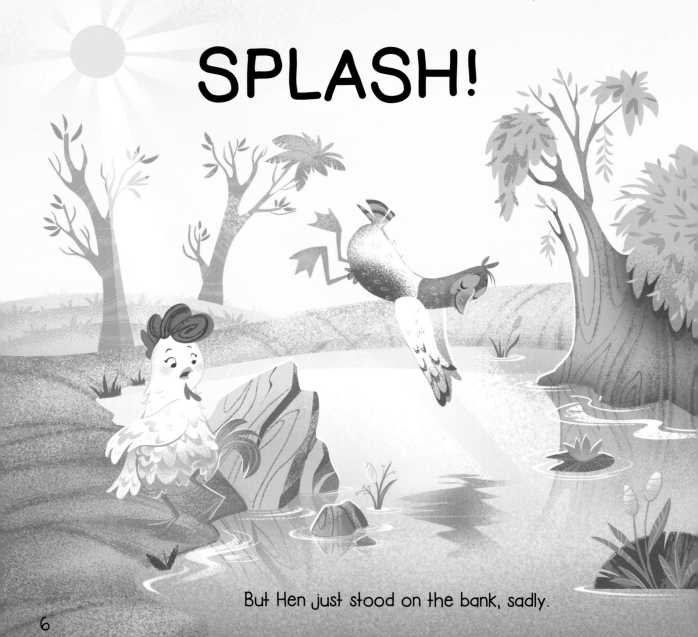

But Hen just stood on the bank, sadly.

I can't swim,

she told everyone.

The other animals giggled and, every time, Duck felt bad for his friend. Then one day, he had a great idea.

Wait here, Hen!

Everyone gathered around the barn.
There were all sorts of funny
noises coming from inside.

CRASH!
BANG!
CLATTER!

Then, the doors
creaked open.

Surprise!
I've made
you a boat!

8

Hen was so happy, she shook her
tail feathers and helped Duck
take the little boat down to the water.

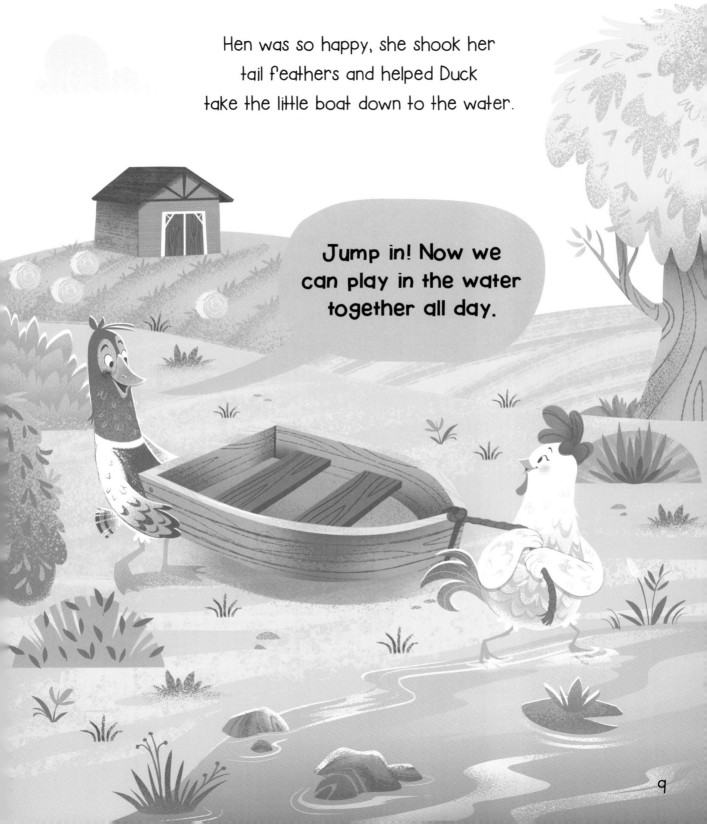

They rowed round and round until they were dizzy and soon, the other animals wanted to join in, too! First they took turns diving off the side.

Then Hen showed everyone
how to water-ski.

Thanks for helping me, Duck. You're the best friend ever!

Chick Learns A Lesson

Chick and Mummy were visiting Horse in the meadow near the wood.

Mummy, what's the wood like?

Mummy told her all about the beautiful flowers
and the animals that lived there.

You must never go there by yourself,

said Mummy, but that just made Chick more curious!

When Mummy wasn't looking, Chick took a tiny step towards the wood.

Nothing bad happened, so she took another.

Just like Mummy said, there were little streams and pretty flowers everywhere. Bunnies **hopped** and squirrels **scampered**. They played chase and hide-and-seek all day.

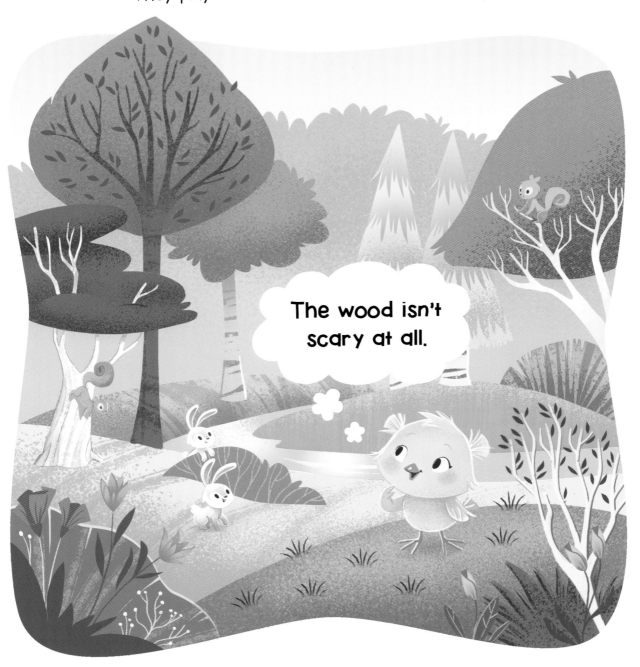

The wood isn't scary at all.

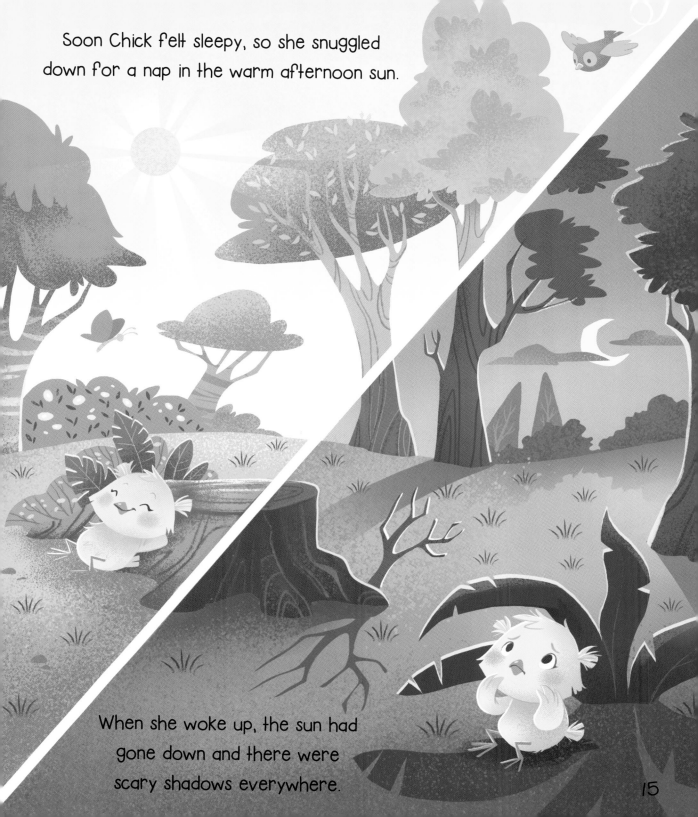

Soon Chick felt sleepy, so she snuggled down for a nap in the warm afternoon sun.

When she woke up, the sun had gone down and there were scary shadows everywhere.

15

Then Chick heard a voice.

Are you lost?

it asked.

Fox appeared from the shadows, grinning with his sharp, shiny teeth. Chick felt very afraid.

Mummy was right. The wood really is scary!

Then she heard a **SQUAWK!** Mummy had come to find her.

No, thank you, Fox. I'll take Chick home.

Little Chick learned a big lesson that day!

Hee-Haw Hamish

Hamish lived with the horses on Sugarlump Farm.
They all had shiny coats and looked so strong as they galloped along.
CLIP-CLOP! Hamish watched them from the field. **HEE-HAW!**

SUGARLUMP FARM

I wish I was special.

The fastest horse of all was Jet.
He loved showing how high he could jump.

The other horses soon had enough of Jet's boasting,
so they trotted far away to graze.

Only Hamish stayed.

Watch this!

Hamish looked on, cheering in amazement. **HEE-HAW!** Suddenly...

SPLAT!

Jet landed in a deep puddle of gloopy mud.

Help, I'm stuck!

cried Jet, looking very worried.

I can't! I'm not strong enough.

Then, Hamish realised there was something he could do that none of the horses could.

21

Hamish took a deep breath and...

HEE-HAW!

HEE-HAW!

He called and yelled until, finally, the other horses galloped across the field.

Fetch some rope. We need to pull out Jet.

The horses tried to pull Jet out, but it was no use.

Hamish, we need your help, too!

Hamish joined in and pulled as hard as he could. At last, Jet was free!

We couldn't have done it without you!

Little Horse's Big Day

Little Horse wanted to go and play with the farm animals for the first time, but Mummy said she needed someone to go with her.

She trotted over to the henhouse.

They look like
a lot of fun!

But the hens were so busy squawking at each other as they
ate their breakfast, they didn't even notice Little Horse.

So Little Horse galloped through the field
to say good morning to the fluffy sheep.

But the flock herded around her in a circle
until she felt quite dizzy. **BAA-BAA!**

She decided to visit the goats instead, but they were having some sort of strange competition.

One flung himself into a huge puddle and mud went all over Little Horse. **SPLAT!**

YUCK!

she cried.

Then, the cows barged past on their way back from milking.
Poor Little Horse was ready to give up.

No one wants to play with me.

Little Horse felt sad and went home to Mummy.

They were just a bit busy. Let me show you around!

The animals **clucked, mooed, baaed** and **cheeped**.

We're sorry. Let's go and have some fun!

Sheep's Secret

Whenever Sheep was on her own,
she loved to sing as loudly as she could.

TRA-LA-BAAAA!

No one else had ever heard her until, one day, a mole popped up.

Sheep's cheeks turned bright red.

Please don't tell anyone. I'd be so embarrassed.

Don't worry. Your secret's safe with me.

Then he dived back underground.

The very same thing happened when Mole found Horse sneaking apples from the goat pen...

... Pig enjoying a quiet bubble bath in the pond...

... and Bunny nibbling on Farmer Kate's flowers.

The next day, Sheep was in the middle of a secret performance. She stopped just in time when she saw Horse coming. But still he said,

I didn't know you liked singing.

Sheep realised Mole must have told Horse her secret, and it wasn't long before everyone else's were out, too!

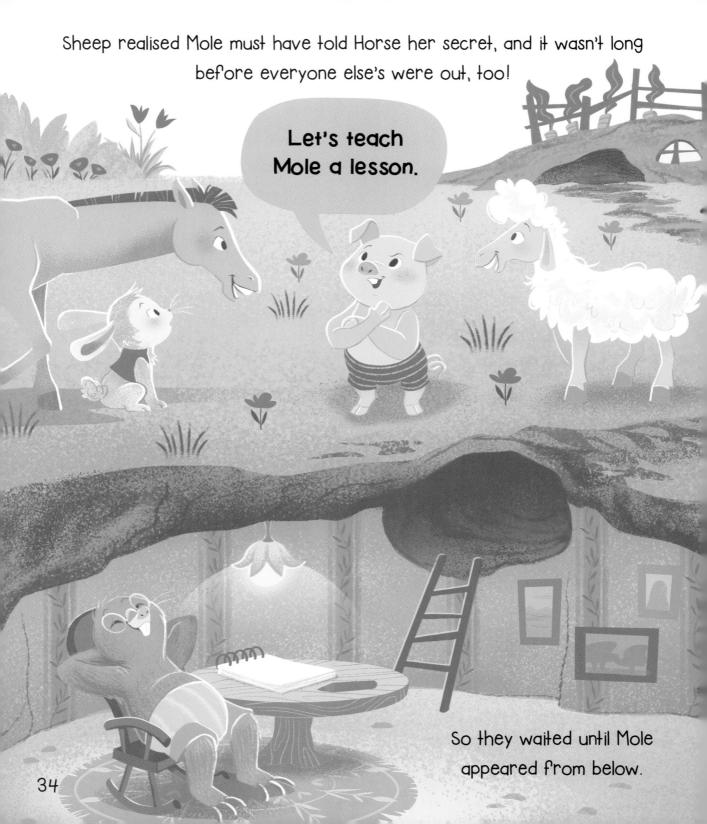

Let's teach Mole a lesson.

So they waited until Mole appeared from below.

The Goat Escape

Little Goat had always wondered what was out in the big, wide world.

I just want some excitement.

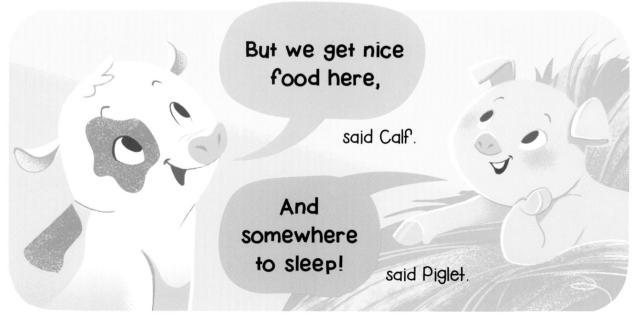

But we get nice food here,

said Calf.

And somewhere to sleep!

said Piglet.

So he went to explore the field on his own,
when he found that the gate was open!

Little Goat sneaked out and was
about to take a big **SLURP**
of water from a trough.

Suddenly...

... BOOM,
BOOM!

bellowed a huge bull.

Quick as a flash, Little Goat scrambled away through the fence.

Then he skipped across the field until his stomach started rumbling.

Little Goat snuffled around for a tasty treat and found a pile of crunchy acorns.

Just as he was about to nibble one, he heard CHITTER-CHATTERING!

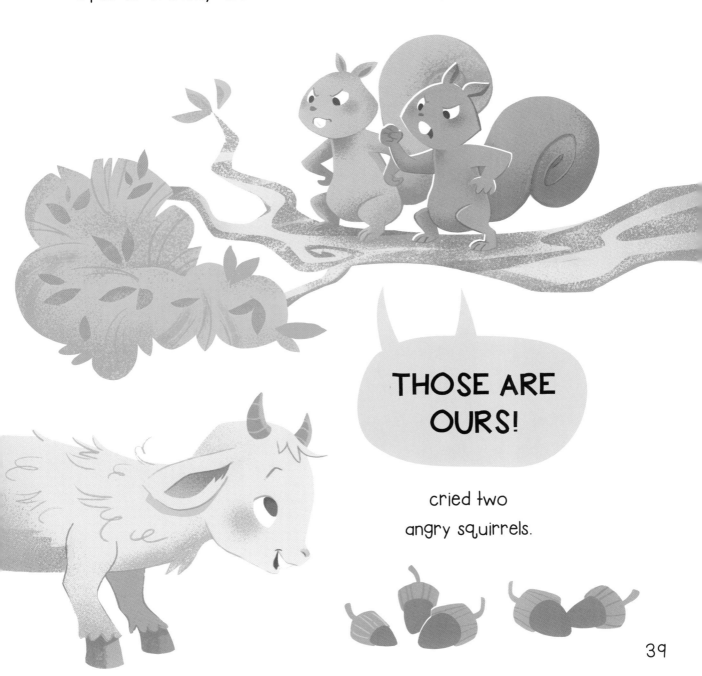

THOSE ARE OURS!

cried two angry squirrels.

The squirrels **snatched** the acorns, so Little Goat looked for somewhere to have a nap. Suddenly, he spotted two little eyes and a long nose.

This is my den,

said a sly fox.

Ahhh!

cried Little Goat.

He raced all the way back to the farm and
everyone was **very** happy to see him.

Little Goat remembered how much he loved his life
on the farm and he **never** ran away again.

Sports Day

The farm animals were bored.

We could learn to juggle?

Or bake mud pies?

Everyone shook their heads.
Then Cow had an idea.

Let's have a sports day!

42

First up was a running race.

Ready, steady,

GO!

shouted Cow.

Horse **galloped** ahead, with Sheep not far behind.
But Mouse's little legs soon got tired.

Here, let
me help.

Horse was in charge of the obstacle course. Goat **darted** over the
hay bales, troughs and milk-pail towers **faster** than anyone,
while Hen **flapped** her wings and flew across them.

SQUAWK!

Pig thought the obstacles were a bit too high
and trotted around them instead.

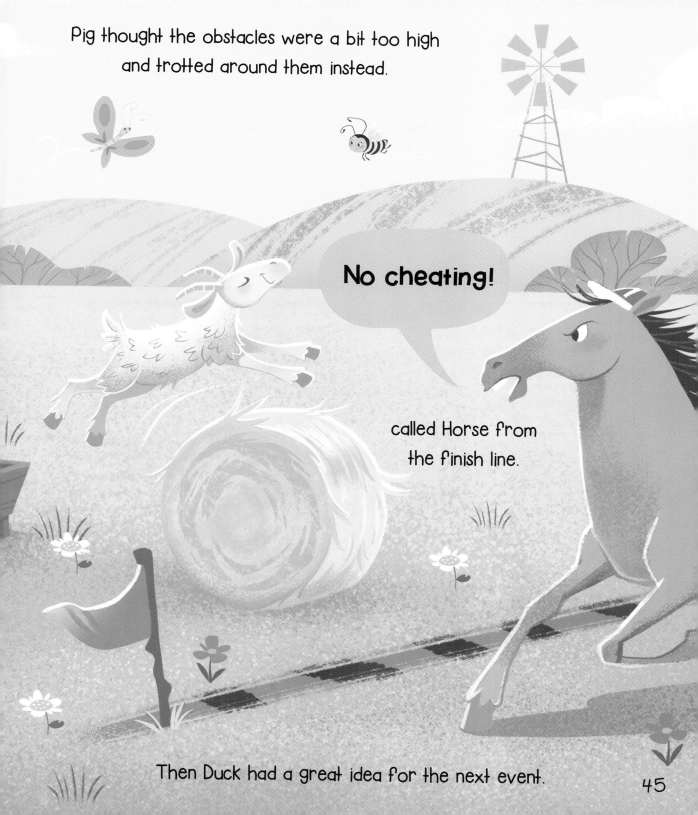

No cheating!

called Horse from
the finish line.

Then Duck had a great idea for the next event.

All the animals headed over to the pond
for a swimming race.

I'll be
the judge,

said Cat, refusing
to get wet.

SPLISH, SPLASH! they went, and Duck and Dog tied for first place.

Finally, Cow put the animals into two teams.

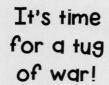

It's time for a tug of war!

They all pulled as hard as they could, but neither team budged. Then, Mouse gave an extra-hard tug...

... SNAP!

The rope broke and the animals tumbled into a heap
on the ground, laughing and giggling.

It's a
draw!

cried Cow.

This had been the best sports day **ever**.